CLEMENTINE ROSE

and the
Famous Friend

Also by Jacqueline Harvey

Clementine Rose and the Surprise Visitor
Clementine Rose and the Pet Day Disaster
Clementine Rose and the Perfect Present
Clementine Rose and the Farm Fiasco
Clementine Rose and the Seaside Escape
Clementine Rose and the Treasure Box
Clementine Rose and the Ballet Break-In

Alice-Miranda at School
Alice-Miranda on Holiday
Alice-Miranda Takes the Lead
Alice-Miranda at Sea
Alice-Miranda in New York
Alice-Miranda Shows the Way
Alice-Miranda in Paris
Alice-Miranda Shines Bright
Alice-Miranda in Japan
Alice-Miranda at Camp

CLEMENTINE ROSE

and the
Famous Friend

Jacqueline Harvey

RED FOX

CLEMENTINE ROSE AND THE FAMOUS FRIEND
A RED FOX BOOK 978 1 849 41877 5

Published in Great Britain by Red Fox,
an imprint of Random House Children's Publishers UK
A Penguin Random House Company

Penguin
Random House
UK

Originally published in Australia by Random House Australia in 2015

This edition published 2016

1 3 5 7 9 10 8 6 4 2

Text copyright © Jacqueline Harvey, 2015

The right of Jacqueline Harvey to be identified as the author of this work
has been asserted in accordance with the Copyright,
Designs and Patents Act 1988.

Penguin Random House is committed to a sustainable future for
our business, our readers and our planet. This book is made from
Forest Stewardship Council® certified paper.

MIX
Paper from
responsible sources
FSC
www.fsc.org   FSC® C018179

Set in ITC Century

RANDOM HOUSE CHILDREN'S PUBLISHERS UK
61–63 Uxbridge Road, London W5 5SA

www.**randomhousechildrens**.co.uk
www.**totallyrandombooks**.co.uk
www.**randomhouse**.co.uk

Addresses for companies within The Random House Group Limited can be
found at: www.randomhouse.co.uk/offices.htm

THE RANDOM HOUSE GROUP Limited Reg. No. 954009

A CIP catalogue record for this book is available from the British Library.

Printed and bound in Great Britain by Clays Ltd, St Ives plc

For Ian, as always, and for
Kimberley, for her unwavering support
and superb editing – 18 books in
four years must be some sort of record.
I will miss you, KB!

MR SMEE

Clementine Rose sat in the front row of the assembly hall. Her schoolmates fidgeted and chatted as a stream of teachers took their seats on the stage. Poppy and Sophie were talking about their holidays but Clementine's new friends, Tilda and Teddy Hobbs, were unusually quiet. The twins and their big sister, Araminta, had moved into the cottage at the end of Clementine's road during the term break. Today was their first day at Ellery Prep and the start of a new school year.

Clementine felt a tug on her sleeve. Tilda pointed at the man sitting at the end of the row of teachers. 'What's his name?'

Clementine shrugged. 'I don't know. I've never seen him before.'

The man wore a smart grey suit and a purple tie with yellow flowers. His wavy, chocolate-coloured hair skimmed the back of his collar. He noticed the girls pointing and smiled at them.

'I think he saw us,' Tilda said with a giggle. 'He looks nice.'

Clementine nodded. 'I like his tie.'

Miss Critchley stepped up to the microphone. Clementine's tummy fluttered but she wasn't nearly as worried as she had been this time last year. This wasn't her first day of Kindergarten – now she was one of the big girls.

The head teacher beamed at the bright-eyed crowd. 'Good morning, children.'

Clementine thought Miss Critchley looked as beautiful as ever in her red dress and matching red heels. Her long brown curls were pulled back into a ponytail.

'Go-ood mor-ning, Miss Critch-ley,' the group chorused.

'I hope you all had a lovely holiday and that you're looking forward to a wonderful year.'

Rows of heads bobbed up and down, like puppets on strings.

'Now, I am sure you're all eager to know who your teachers will be,' Miss Critchley said. She looked at the front row of students. 'I can hardly believe you're in Year One – it only seems like yesterday that I was welcoming you into Kindergarten. Who can remember last year, when you met Mrs Bottomley?'

'Who could forget Bossy Boots Bottomley?' Joshua blurted.

Laughter spread like a wave through the assembly hall.

Angus Archibald poked Joshua in the ribs. 'That's my nan you're talking about.'

Miss Critchley gave them an icy stare. 'Boys, that's quite enough.'

Clementine looked at the row of teachers and wondered where Mrs Bottomley was. She was probably getting things ready for the new Kindergarten class, Clementine decided.

A hand shot up in the second row.

'Yes, Nigel?' said Miss Critchley.

The boy pointed at the man with the purple-and-yellow tie. 'Who's that?'

'I was just about to introduce Mr Smee,' said Miss Critchley. She motioned for the man to join her at the microphone. 'Children, this is Mr Roderick Smee and he's going to be teaching . . .' She paused. 'Year One.'

There was a gasp from the children in the front row.

'Yes!' Joshua pumped his fist in the air. 'A boy teacher.'

'That I am,' Mr Smee replied with a grin.

'Mr Smee has lots of experience,' said Miss Critchley. She looked straight at Joshua and Angus and wiggled her eyebrows. 'So don't go thinking that he's a pushover just because he smiles a lot.'

The Year One students nodded.

'Could you tell us a few things about yourself,

Mr Smee?' asked Miss Critchley. 'It's lovely for the children to get to know the teachers.'

'Well, I play the guitar and I like making movies, and reading is just about one of the best things you can do,' said the man with a big smile. 'And I can't wait to meet everyone in Year One.'

The children watched him, wide-eyed.

'He's cool,' said Joshua Tribble. It came out much louder than he had intended.

Mr Smee winked. 'Thanks, buddy.'

Joshua's ears turned pink and he covered his mouth.

'I think you have some very excited students, Mr Smee. Year One, seeing that you know everyone else on stage, I'd like you to stand and follow Astrid outside. Mr Smee will meet you in a minute.' Miss Critchley smiled at Astrid, who was sitting at the end of the row, nearest the door. The girl led the group out into the morning sunshine. In less than a minute the children had organised themselves into alphabetical order, with Astrid helping

Tilda and Tom to find their places in the line.

Mr Smee arrived and cast his eyes over the class. 'Wow! You're very well organised.'

'We're in alphabetical order,' Clementine announced.

'No!' He frowned in disbelief.

'Yes, we are,' Clementine reassured him. 'You can test us.'

Mr Smee looked at the children, wondering how on earth a group of five- and six-year-olds had managed to arrange themselves into alphabetical order.

He pointed to the curly-haired lad at the head of the line. 'Okay then, what's your name?'

'Angus Archibald,' the boy replied.

Mr Smee then pointed at the girl behind him, Astrid, who was followed by Clementine. He could hardly believe his ears as he ticked off each child. He smiled broadly. 'That's amazing. But you don't have to line up in alphabetical order for me. In fact,' he lowered his voice, 'I'll let you in on a secret. I'm not really a big fan of lines at all.'

7

The children suddenly stiffened, their backs straight and arms jammed beside their bodies.

Mr Smee gawped. This was not the usual reaction to his little secret. Then he noticed that the children weren't looking at him at all. He turned around to see Ethel Bottomley striding towards them, dressed from tip to toe in her trademark brown.

'Good morning, Mrs Bottomley,' the class sang.

'Good morning, everyone.' The old woman cast a stern eye over the group.

'Did *you* teach them to line up like that, Mrs Bottomley?' Mr Smee asked.

She nodded. 'I certainly did. I think you will find that these are the most well-disciplined students in the school and I will thank you not to go ruining them with your hippy ideas.'

She'd met the young man at the staff meeting the day before and was horrified to hear some of the plans he outlined for the children.

8

Roderick Smee worked hard to smother a grin. 'Of course not, Mrs Bottomley.' It wasn't entirely true, but there was no point upsetting her.

He looked back to the students and gave the barest hint of a wink. 'Come on, Year One. Time to get excited about learning.'

'Excited?' Mrs Bottomley could hardly believe her ears. 'Mr Smee, I think you should choose your words far more carefully or these children will be running amok in no time.'

Clementine held Tilda's hand and gave it a squeeze. It seemed that Year One was going to be a lot more fun than Kindergarten.

AN UNEXPECTED GUEST

Clementine Rose clattered through the front door. She kicked off her school shoes and ran down the hallway to the kitchen, skidding along the polished timber boards on her socks.

'Mummy, we're home!'

She pushed her way through the kitchen door and dropped her backpack by the sideboard.

Lady Clarissa Appleby was stirring a large pot on the stove. The house smelt like warm apples and cinnamon. Clementine grinned. Her mother was probably making a pie. Aunt Violet was sitting at the table with her head buried in a fashion magazine.

'Hello darling.' Lady Clarissa smiled at her little daughter. Clementine's blue eyes sparkled like sapphires and she wore a huge grin. 'It looks like someone's had a good day.'

'Oh Mummy, it was the best ever. Our teacher's name is Mr Smee and he's very funny and he had a lovely tie with yellow flowers,' Clementine babbled. She scurried into her mother's embrace and the woman kissed the top of her golden head.

Aunt Violet lowered her magazine and tapped her forefinger against her powdered cheek. 'Don't I get a greeting? Or are you too old, now that you're in Year One?'

'Of course not.' Clementine raced around the table and leaned in to kiss Aunt Violet.

Digby Pertwhistle arrived in the kitchen, holding Clementine's school shoes in one hand and a shopping bag in the other.

'Uncle Digby, what are you doing with those?' Lady Clarissa took the offending footwear and looked at Clementine. 'Darling, you know you can't leave shoes lying about in the foyer. If one of the guests trips over them we'll be in all sorts of trouble.'

'Sorry, Mummy.' Clementine took the shoes from her mother and set them down beside the back stairs. Lavender, her teacup pig, and Aunt Violet's sphynx cat, Pharaoh, were sound asleep in Lavender's basket in front of the oven. Clementine gave both pets a scratch under the chin. Lavender let out a loud grunt and Pharaoh began to purr, but neither creature opened an eye.

'Would you like something to eat, Clementine?' Uncle Digby offered as he unpacked the groceries on the bench.

'Yes, please. I'm starving.'

She had just clambered onto the chair beside Aunt Violet when she remembered something important and slid back down again. Clementine went to her backpack and took out a large pile of exercise books. She heaved them onto the table then climbed back onto the chair.

Aunt Violet shook her head. 'Are you a jack-in-the-box?'

'No,' Clementine said. 'I just remembered that Mr Smee said we should cover all our books tonight.'

'Well, I hope you're not expecting me to do it,' Aunt Violet said, her lip curling.

Clementine shook her head. 'No. Uncle Digby's much better at it than you. Remember last time when you tried? There were big air bubbles everywhere and we had to prick them with a pin. Mrs Bottomley got cross at me and said that it looked like a hippopotamus had tried to cover my books. But I told her it was just you.'

'Pfft.' Aunt Violet went back to reading her magazine.

'Oh dear. I hope we have enough paper,' Lady Clarissa said.

'We've got plenty. I picked some up from Mrs Mogg,' said Uncle Digby.

'You're a gem.' Lady Clarissa smiled at the man, who was now busy making a glass of chocolate milk for Clementine.

He set the glass and a plate with two honey jumbles in front of her. She took a large gulp of milk and then exhaled loudly, leaving a chocolate moustache on her upper lip.

Aunt Violet blanched. 'Do you have any manners, young lady?'

Clementine wiped her mouth with the back of her hand. Aunt Violet shook her head.

Lady Clarissa laughed and sat opposite her daughter. 'So, tell us about Mr Smee.'

'Oh Mummy, he's amazing. He taught us songs and played the guitar and he doesn't like lining up. I don't think Mrs Bottomley was very happy about that,' Clementine explained.

'Poor Ethel,' said Aunt Violet. 'That woman worked hard to get your class shipshape last year. I'm sure she'll be very upset if this upstart comes along and undoes all her good work.'

Clementine ploughed on. 'We don't have rows any more, either. There are lots of big

14

tables instead. My table has Poppy and Sophie and Tilda and Teddy and Angus and we're called the Warthogs.'

'Warthogs! That's dreadful,' Aunt Violet scoffed.

'No, that's what we wanted to be. Tilda and Teddy told everyone about Theodore and they all agreed that it would be cool to be the Warthogs,' Clementine explained. Theodore was the stuffed warthog that used to live in the Penberthy House library but was now safely tucked away in the attic. 'The other tables are called Flamingos, Wildebeests and Cheetahs. We're all named after African animals.'

The conversation was interrupted by the tinkling of a bell in a box near the pantry.

Long ago, even before Aunt Violet was born, the house had been full of servants. A series of buttons throughout the house had allowed the occupants to summon the servants whenever they wanted anything. Lady Clarissa had recently had the bells and buttons restored. They were strictly for the use of guests, although Aunt Violet had tried them out several times when she was after a cup of tea and couldn't be bothered to walk downstairs.

The bell rang again.

'Is someone staying?' Clementine asked, surprised that there was a guest at the beginning of the week. The hotel was always busiest at the weekends.

'Yes, darling,' her mother replied, pushing her chair out.

'She seems an odd little woman if you ask me,' Aunt Violet said. 'Is she really staying the whole month?'

Lady Clarissa nodded. 'Miss Richardson has paid up-front. She didn't have to, but she insisted. She said that she might stay longer if things suit her.'

'That's a long time,' said Clementine. She finished her last bite of honey jumble and pushed her chair out too. 'Can I come and meet her, Mummy? I could bring Lavender.'

'No, darling. Why don't you stay down here and help Uncle Digby get started with your books? I've got some lovely labels in the second drawer of the sideboard. I'll be back soon.' Lady Clarissa rushed away up the back stairs.

'Why did you say the lady was odd, Aunt Violet?' Clementine asked. She wondered if the woman looked strange or if she talked to herself. The other week Clementine had seen a man in the village with a glass eye. She'd gasped and hidden behind her mother's skirt. The man had explained that it wasn't anything to be worried about and in the end Clementine thought it was amazing.

'She's come to write a book,' Aunt Violet replied, 'but I don't imagine she'll find Penberthy Floss very inspiring.'

Clementine's face lit up. She loved stories and was getting very good with her reading. At the moment her favourite book was by a lady called Agnes Wells. She'd been taking turns reading a chapter each evening with Aunt Violet, who seemed to be enjoying the story just as much as Clementine was. She said that it reminded her of things she'd read as a little girl, but Clementine didn't think it was old-fashioned. It was a great adventure. 'What sort of book?' Clementine asked.

Aunt Violet flicked her hand. 'Some historical tome. I'd never heard of Abigail Richardson and you know I'm *very* widely read. It all sounds dreadfully dull to me.'

But Clementine didn't think it was dull at all. She couldn't wait to meet the lady who was writing a book in her very own house.

THE
WRITER

When Lady Clarissa returned from upstairs, she and Clementine walked to the village to collect the mail. They stopped to look at the progress on the village hall, which had recently been destroyed in a fire. Clementine was excited to see that there was already a floor and a frame. That meant that Tilda and Teddy's mother, Ana, would be able to start her ballet school soon. Clementine couldn't wait to have lessons. Mrs Mogg was going to make her a red tutu.

By the time they arrived back, Uncle Digby had covered most of Clementine's books and dinner was well underway. Aunt Violet had gone upstairs to have a rest, complaining that she had a headache coming on.

Clementine settled down to colour in the title page in her writing book. Her pencils spilled out of their pretty pink polka-dot case all over the kitchen table.

'Clemmie, can you pack your things away and set the table for me, please?' Lady Clarissa asked as she strained a large saucepan of vegetables.

'Is the writer lady having dinner with us?' Clementine asked as she bundled up her pencils. She hadn't seen Uncle Digby set the table in the dining room, which was where the guests usually ate their meals.

'No, darling. Miss Richardson has asked to have dinner taken up to her room,' Lady Clarissa replied.

'She's a bit *'sterious*,' Clementine said.

Aunt Violet walked down the back stairs into the kitchen at that moment.

'"Mysterious" is the word you're looking for, Clementine,' she said as she strode over to the table. 'You're a big girl now. You need to start pronouncing your words correctly or I'll enrol you in some elocution lessons.'

Clementine stopped in her tracks. 'Electrocution lessons! What's that?' Clementine's mother and Uncle Digby had always told her to stay away from electricity because it was dangerous.

Lady Clarissa and Uncle Digby laughed.

'Godfathers, Clementine. Elocution, not electrocution. It means learning how to speak properly. Given you're so fond of all those silly poems Pertwhistle insists on teaching you, it would be a very good idea,' said Aunt Violet.

Clementine sighed with relief.

'Aunt Violet, that's a lovely thought but I'm afraid my budget won't stretch to soccer, ballet and elocution at the moment. Why don't you teach Clementine? I'm sure she'd enjoy learning some more poems from you as well,' Lady Clarissa teased.

'Clarissa, I'm no teacher and thank heavens for that,' Aunt Violet said with a shudder. 'You should hear some of the horrendous tales Mrs Bottomley has shared with me. No, Pertwhistle can keep instructing her and I'll just correct them when necessary.'

'Of course she will,' Uncle Digby whispered. He gave Clementine a wink and she smothered a giggle.

Clementine was trying to imagine Aunt Violet standing out the front of her class. She shivered just thinking about it.

'Oh, Clarissa.' Uncle Digby turned from where he was stirring a pot on the stove. 'I've just remembered that we're low on candles in the dining room. We'll need them for Friday night. You might want to add them to the shopping list.'

'Thanks, Uncle Digby,' said Clarissa. 'I think we're almost out of chocolates too.' She wiped her hands on her apron and dashed over to the sideboard to add the items to her never-ending shopping list.

'Do you think I could tell the guests one of my poems at the special dinner?' Clementine asked.

'Let's just see how things go,' Lady Clarissa replied. 'Not everyone appreciates your poems as much as Granny and Grandpa and Uncle Digby and I do.'

'What special dinner?' Aunt Violet asked.

'Aunt Violet, you remember that Uncle Digby suggested we offer a dining package with the family as part of a weekend stay?' Lady Clarissa reminded the woman.

'No! That sounds perfectly ghastly.'

'You were there, Aunt Violet. You groaned about it when Mummy told you and you said that you'd rather eat in the kitchen with Lavender and Pharaoh than have to entertain any silly guests,' Clementine said.

Aunt Violet huffed. 'Well, what of it?'

'We're having our first dinner this week,' Lady Clarissa explained as she drained and mashed the potatoes.

The old woman put the back of her hand

on her forehead. 'I think I can feel a fever coming on.'

'Oh no, Aunt Violet, I don't think so,' Clarissa chided. 'I need you to be there.'

Aunt Violet sighed. 'And what do I get out of it?'

'A lovely dinner and the pleasure of our company,' Lady Clarissa said with a grin.

'And maybe a poem too,' Clementine said with a smile.

Aunt Violet rolled her eyes. 'Oh, lucky me.'

Lady Clarissa scooped the last of the mashed potato onto the fifth plate while Uncle Digby poured a trail of gravy over the top of the roast chicken and vegetables.

He placed one of the plates onto a large tray, along with a pair of crystal salt and pepper shakers and a tall glass with a bottle of mineral water beside it.

'Please may I help, Uncle Digby?' asked Clementine. She rushed over to see what she might carry.

'No, it's fine, Clemmie. I'll be back in a jiffy

and we can have our dinner,' he said, and set off upstairs.

Clementine frowned. 'Will I *ever* get to meet Miss Richardson?'

'She's very busy with her work, darling. I don't want you to interrupt her and I'm sure you'll get to meet her when she's ready,' said Lady Clarissa.

'She's no one special, Clementine,' Aunt Violet said. 'I told you that before. Don't go thinking we've got anyone famous up there.'

After dinner, Pharaoh and Lavender wandered over to Clemmie for their nightly tummy tickles. Both creatures rolled about on the flagstone floor, enjoying all the attention. Lady Clarissa had gone upstairs to run Clementine a bath.

'Well, the washing up won't do itself,' Uncle Digby declared as he stood up to clear the last of the plates.

Aunt Violet rose too. 'You'll have to manage it on your own, Pertwhistle. My head is pounding. It must be the thought of that wretched dinner.'

Clementine looked up at her great-aunt. 'Your head is always pounding when it's time to do the washing up, Aunt Violet. Are you allergic?'

Uncle Digby glanced over his shoulder with a knowing look.

'Don't be ridiculous, Clementine,' said the old woman. She stalked across the room and disappeared up the back stairs.

'I'll wipe up, Uncle Digby,' Clementine offered. She ran off to wash her hands first.

'Good girl,' said Uncle Digby.

Just as Clementine picked up a clean tea towel the front doorbell rang.

Digby glanced at the kitchen clock. It was almost seven. 'I wonder who that could be. Unless it's our wine delivery. He should have been here hours ago.'

'I'll go,' Clementine offered.

'No, you stay here.' The old man took off

27

his yellow rubber gloves and hurried from the room.

A few seconds later another bell tinkled by the pantry. Clementine looked at the old-fashioned light box above the pantry door. Each light was labelled with the name of a room in the house. It could only be Aunt Violet or Miss Richardson ringing the bell. The light for the Rose Room was glowing. The bell rang again.

Clementine ran out into the hall to find Uncle Digby. He was standing at the open front door talking to a man in overalls.

'Sorry it's so late but there was an accident on the motorway,' the man said gruffly.

'Why don't you drive around to the garage and I'll help you unload it,' said Uncle Digby.

He walked out the door and closed it behind him.

Clementine frowned and scurried back into the kitchen to see if her mother had returned, but there was no sign of her. The bell rang again.

There was only one thing to do. Clementine

scampered up the back stairs and along the corridor.

She tapped gently on the door of the Rose Room. There was no answer. She opened the door and poked her head inside.

'Hello Miss Richardson?' Clementine said. 'May I help you?'

'Who are you?' a high voice wavered from deep inside the room. 'Where's Miss Appleby?'

The Rose Room was the largest bedroom in the house with a four-poster bed in the centre and a small dining table for two in one corner. A roll-top writing desk with carved legs stood behind the enormous bed, by one of the windows. There was a huge wardrobe and an ensuite bathroom too. The Rose Room had received the most attention over the years and was by far the loveliest of all.

Clementine couldn't see where the voice was coming from. 'Excuse me, Miss Richardson, but where are you?' she asked as she walked into the room.

'S-s-stop right there,' the voice stuttered. 'What is your name and why are you here?'

'I'm Clementine and I live here.'

'Nobody told me there were children. Are you the only one?' The woman sounded nervous and a bit cross too.

'Yes, except when I have friends over to play. Sometimes I have sleepovers with Poppy and Sophie, and Jules comes too,' Clementine explained.

'Why did you come? Where's your mother?'

'She's running my bath and Aunt Violet has gone to bed with a headache, but that's just because she didn't want to do the washing up. Uncle Digby was answering the front door and helping the man with a delivery, so there was only me left,' said Clementine.

'Go away. I don't want to see you. I don't want to see any children at all.'

'Why?' Clementine asked.

'I have my reasons.'

'Aunt Violet doesn't like children very much either but I think I've grown on her – at least, that's what Mrs Mogg said to Mummy,' Clementine said.

'I didn't say that I don't *like* children,' the woman said, her voice softening a little.

Clementine frowned in confusion. 'I just came to see what you wanted. If it's a cup of tea you'll have to wait for Uncle Digby because I'm not allowed to make it yet. But if you want a glass of water or a biscuit or a piece of cake, I could get that. So long as I don't have to use the big knife.'

She craned her neck around the nearest bedpost. At last she spotted the woman. Miss Richardson was sitting at the writing desk but Clementine could only see the top of her grey head.

'I don't want anything. Now off you go,' said Miss Richardson. She still hadn't turned around.

Clementine was about to ask Miss Richardson about her book when she heard her mother calling her name.

'What are you waiting for? Shoo!' the old woman quavered.

Clementine reversed out of the room and closed the door.

'Clemmie, what were you doing in there?' Lady Clarissa demanded. She had searched everywhere for the girl.

'Miss Richardson rang the bell and Uncle Digby had gone to see who was at the front door and Aunt Violet had gone to bed so there was only me.'

'Did you find out what Miss Richardson wanted?' Lady Clarissa asked.

Clementine shook her head. 'She wouldn't tell me. I don't think she likes children much.'

'Oh dear. Go upstairs and hop into the bath while see what I can do here. I'm sure that Miss Richardson has her reasons for not wanting to talk to you. You just have to remember that not all grown-ups are fond of children,' said Lady Clarissa.

Clementine nodded. 'I know that. I live with Aunt Violet.'

A PROJECT

By Friday morning Clementine hadn't seen any more of the mysterious Miss Richardson. She had tried to accompany her mother or Uncle Digby to deliver trays of food or freshly washed clothes to the woman, but she was sent away each time. As the week wore on more guests came to stay, so Lady Clarissa and Uncle Digby were kept very busy. Aunt Violet was left in charge of getting Clementine to and from school each day.

'Do you think there's something wrong with

34

Miss Richardson?' Clementine asked from the back seat of Aunt Violet's shiny red car as they sped towards school on Friday morning. 'Maybe she's allergic to sunshine or something.' Clementine gasped. 'Maybe she's a vampire!'

Clementine had heard of vampires only recently. Tilda and Teddy were so disappointed that there were no ghosts at Penberthy House that Teddy decided there might be vampires instead. Clementine didn't believe it. She'd never seen any bats in the house.

Aunt Violet tutted as her eyes met Clementine's in the rear-vision mirror. 'A vampire? What nonsense are you talking about now? I suspect she's simply suffering from a bout of self-importance.'

'What do you mean?' the child asked.

'Well, she came to write a book, didn't she? She must think it's frightfully important for her to stay in that room working all day and night. I don't think it's very healthy and certainly not at all sociable, and as for the number of times she rings that bell of hers – she's had us all running up and down those stairs like mad monkeys.' Aunt Violet pouted and pulled into the kerb at the front of the school. 'Have a good day, Clementine.'

'You know you're not supposed to park here,' Clementine said, pointing at the NO STOPPING sign.

'I'm not parking. I'm dropping. Now hurry up and get out,' said Aunt Violet.

Clementine leaned forward between the seats and pecked her great-aunt's powdery cheek. 'See you this afternoon.' She hopped out of the car, shut the door with a bang and raced away.

'How many times do I have to tell you not to slam the door!' the old woman yelled.

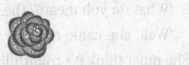

Clementine and her fellow Warthogs tumbled into the classroom after lunch and went straight to their desks. They couldn't wait to hear what Mr Smee had in store for them. That morning he'd taught them a new song, they'd had a run around the obstacle course on the oval and finished two pages of sums. The work was definitely harder than in Kindergarten but Clementine couldn't remember loving school as much as she had in the past week.

'Year One, I have to give it to Mrs Bottomley, she certainly has taught you well,' Mr Smee said as he looked out at his eager students. 'I've decided to set you a project. It will be challenging, but I think you'll find it fun. And school *should* be fun, shouldn't it?' he asked with a smile.

The students looked at one another in delight. Mrs Bottomley had never mentioned 'fun' in the classroom.

Angus Archibald raised his hand. Mr Smee nodded.

'What's a project?' Angus asked.

'Does anyone know?' Mr Smee scanned the room. Hands shot up all over the place. 'Yes, Teddy?'

'It's when you do research,' said the boy.

Mr Smee nodded. 'Very good.'

'What's research?' Joshua called out.

'Did you forget something?' Mr Smee looked at the lad closely. Joshua quickly put his hand up. Mr Smee grinned. 'Yes, Joshua?'

'What's research?' the boy asked.

'Would anyone like to explain?'

Astrid's hand was already in the air. The teacher pointed to her. 'Research is where you find out facts about things. Then you have to write a report or do a presentation with those facts. That's the project part,' she answered.

Mr Smee nodded. 'Very good. I want you to think about someone you admire. It might be a person who has invented something or plays sport or your favourite author or someone in the community who makes a difference. They don't have to be famous but it's probably simpler if they are, because then it will be easier to look them up. Once you have collected some interesting facts about your chosen person, you will give a talk pretending you're that person.'

Angus's face scrunched up. 'I don't get it.'

'Yeah,' Joshua butted in. 'How can you be someone else?'

'Put up your hand if you've ever pretended to be another person? Maybe a superhero or a king or a queen?' the teacher asked.

Twenty hands shot into the air.

'Ooh. Batman!' Joshua called out.

Mr Smee stared at the boy, who raised his hand too.

'Well, instead of just imagining what it's like to be someone else, this time you have to find out some important things about the person you choose. Then you can dress up like them and give a short talk pretending that you are them,' Mr Smee said. 'Yes, Astrid?'

'If I chose Queen Georgiana, I could dress up like her and say, "Good evening, royal subjects".' Astrid spoke with a funny posh voice and the children giggled. 'Is that what you mean?'

Mr Smee smiled. 'That's exactly what I mean.'

'Can I be my mum?' asked Tilda.

'She's not famous,' Joshua scoffed. 'She's just a boring mum.'

Clementine turned around and faced the boy. 'Mums aren't boring and Tilda's mum was a ballerina.'

'No, she wasn't,' the boy retorted.

'It's true. Mummy was a famous dancer,' said Tilda.

'I think you'll find, Joshua, that Anastasia Barkov was the principal dancer with the Royal Ballet for many years,' said Mr Smee.

Joshua looked from Tilda to the teacher. 'But I thought her mum's name was Mrs Hobbs.'

'That raises an interesting point, doesn't it?' said Mr Smee. 'Some famous people use different names for their work. Writers do that a lot and so do actors.'

'That's stupid,' Joshua declared. 'When I'm a movie star I'm going to be Joshua Tribble.'

'Well, it's a name no one will forget,' Mr Smee said with a grin. 'So . . . choose your person over the weekend and on Monday we'll start researching. I've asked Miss Critchley if Year

41

One can be in charge of assembly the week after that. We'll invite your parents in and you can present your work to the whole school.'

'Oh!' the children gasped.

'Mrs Bottomley only let us sing a song once at assembly last year and it was really boring,' Joshua said. 'It was about parsley and sage and someone called Rosemary who couldn't tell the time.'

Mr Smee laughed. 'Do you mean "Scarborough Fair"?'

The children nodded.

He remembered singing that when he was a boy. 'That's a lovely old song,' he said, almost feeling sorry for Mrs Bottomley. Perhaps he could give her some newer material that the children might know.

'We'll be famous,' Angus blurted.

'Well, famous at Ellery Prep,' said Mr Smee.

'Cool,' Joshua said. 'I'm Batman.'

'Batman's not real, Joshua,' Teddy called.

'Yes, he is,' the boy snapped.

'It's okay, Joshua. I can help you with some ideas,' Mr Smee offered.

'This is going to be fun,' Clementine announced. The rest of the Warthogs nodded.

'I have a note for you to take home tonight so you can talk to your parents about your famous friend,' Mr Smee concluded.

'Is that what we're calling the project?' Astrid asked.

'You know, Astrid, in the past I've called the project "My Hero", but I really like "My Famous Friend". Let's put it to a vote.'

Mr Smee hadn't noticed Ethel Bottomley standing in the doorway. She was listening intently and watching the man's every move.

'Who'd like to call our special project "My Famous Friend"?' the teacher asked.

Most of the children raised their hands.

'Who votes for "My Hero"?'

Joshua, Angus and three other students put their hands up.

'That's it then,' said Mr Smee. 'My Famous Friend it is.'

'*Oh,*' Joshua whined. 'Heroes are much better. Like Batman.'

Mrs Bottomley had seen quite enough. She knocked loudly on the doorframe.

The children immediately sat up straighter and folded their arms in front of them.

'Hello Mrs Bottomley,' Mr Smee greeted her. 'What can I do for you?'

'I hadn't realised Year One was a democracy,' the old woman griped. She pinched her lips together as if she'd just sucked a lemon.

'Oh yes,' the man replied. 'Just wait until you see what the children have in store for you in a couple of weeks' time.'

'I shudder to think. I suspect by then they'll be in charge of the classroom, with you tied to your chair, blindfolded and a . . . a . . . a pumpkin balanced on your head!' she exclaimed.

There was a gasp as the children watched Mrs Bottomley turn on her sensible brown heels and march out the door.

'Oops,' Mr Smee said with a grimace. He wondered if there was a reason she'd come to the door or if she was simply spying on him.

'Don't worry about her, Mr Smee,' Clementine said. 'Mrs Bottomley barks more than she bites.'

'Well, that's a relief.' The teacher gave Clementine an embarrassed grin. He was imagining just how big a pumpkin might fit on top of his head.

SMASH

lementine and her friends hurried to the school gate where lots of parents were milling about waiting for their children. She scanned the crowd, searching for Aunt Violet, but there was no sign of her. It wasn't long until there was just Clementine, Tilda, Teddy and Araminta Hobbs left standing with Mrs Bottomley, who was on duty.

'Who's picking you up today, Clementine?' the teacher asked.

'It's supposed to be Aunt Violet but she must be running late,' Clementine replied with a shrug.

Mrs Bottomley looked down at her watch. 'I hope she's not too much longer. I have an appointment at the hairdresser.'

'But your hair always looks the same,' Clementine commented.

'Yes, that's because I have regular appointments. What about you lot?' Mrs Bottomley looked at Araminta and the twins.

'Daddy's coming, I think,' the older girl said.

The woman frowned. 'Well, he'd better hurry up too.'

In the distance the children spied a red car speeding towards them. It screeched to a halt and Aunt Violet hopped out and walked around to the footpath.

'You're a bit late, Violet,' Mrs Bottomley said tersely.

'Ethel, you have no idea,' Aunt Violet blustered, ignoring her friend's tetchiness. 'We have a very demanding guest at the moment and Clarissa and Pertwhistle have been so distracted that I've been running up and down stairs to the woman, seeing to her every need. She rings that bell more often than a door-to-door salesman. But I'm not allowed to use mine – even when I've got a bad head, all I get is ignored!'

'Poor you,' Mrs Bottomley commented. 'Perhaps you'd like to spend a day with Kindergarten instead?'

'Godfathers, not in this lifetime. Although apparently I'm running a car pool for half the village.' The old woman cast her eyes towards the Hobbs children.

'Oh good, are you taking them with you?' Mrs Bottomley asked. She was thinking that she might just make her hair appointment after all.

'Yes,' Aunt Violet huffed.

'Why are you late, Aunt Violet?' Clementine asked.

'And hello to you too. Come along Hobbses, you're coming with us,' said Aunt Violet, turning

48

her attention to the three children standing by the fence.

Clementine's eyes lit up.

Araminta frowned. 'But Daddy said he'd pick us up on his way home from the city.'

'It seems that your parents have been delayed. They'll drop over and get you in a little while,' Aunt Violet said. 'I'll see you for bridge next week, Ethel.' Aunt Violet turned back around but Mrs Bottomley had already fled. 'Good heavens! What's happened to everyone's manners today?'

Teddy wrenched open the back door of the car and launched his backpack across the seat. 'Can we play with Lavender when we get home?'

'Excuse me, young man! I don't know how you treat your parents' car, but in mine bags go in the boot, if you don't mind,' Aunt Violet said tersely.

Teddy sheepishly crawled across the seat and retrieved the offending item, which Aunt Violet snatched off him.

49

'We can play with Lavender and Pharaoh too,' Clementine said, trying to make Teddy feel better.

The children piled into the back of the car. Araminta sat next to Aunt Violet, who turned the key in the ignition and revved the engine.

'Has everyone got their seatbelts on?' Araminta asked as she realised the old woman was about to drive off without checking.

'Oh, yes, hurry up,' Aunt Violet said. 'I have to stop at Pierre's. Why he couldn't have delivered everything this afternoon is beyond me. What do I look like? A courier?'

'Pierre's? Yum!' Clementine exclaimed. 'May we have something for afternoon tea?'

'Don't push your luck, Clementine,' Aunt Violet said as she sped away from the kerb and down the street.

Aunt Violet pulled up outside the shop and was surprised to see Pierre standing on the footpath holding two large cake boxes.

'Bonjour, Madam Appleby,' he said with a smile as the woman hopped out of the car. 'I 'ave everything ready for you. Monsieur

Pertwhistle telephoned ahead and said that you would 'ave the children, so it is much easier for me to come out to you. And I am so sorry I could not make the delivery. My van is being repaired.'

'Oh. Well, thank you, Pierre,' Aunt Violet replied. His gesture seemed to take the wind right out of her sails.

Clementine put the window down so she could say hello.

'I 'ope you don't mind but I have included some treats for the youngsters.' Pierre looked at Clementine and gave her a wink.

Clementine clapped her hands together. 'Thank you, Pierre,' she called.

The man placed the boxes in the boot and made sure they were securely positioned with the schoolbags around them.

'Bon appétit, children!' Pierre grinned and gave a wave as Aunt Violet hopped back into the car. Clementine and the Hobbs children waved back as Aunt Violet drove away.

'Pierre's so thoughtful,' said Clementine.

Tilda nodded. 'And he makes the best cakes.'

The children chatted as Aunt Violet concentrated on the road ahead.

'Who are you going to do your project on, Clementine?' Tilda asked.

'I don't know,' she replied.

'What's this about a project?' Aunt Violet asked.

'It's called My Famous Friend,' Tilda offered. 'I'm doing mine about Mummy.'

'And I'm going to do Daddy,' said Teddy.

'Clementine, what about you?' Aunt Violet asked.

'I don't know.' She shook her head. 'There's no one famous in our family.'

'Does the person have to be famous?' Aunt Violet asked, glancing in the rear-vision mirror at the children in the back seat.

'They have to be someone we admire and look up to,' Teddy explained.

'Well,' said Aunt Violet. 'Isn't there someone in the family you admire and look up to, Clementine?'

'Mummy and Grandpa, but they're not famous. I wonder if Miss Richardson is famous. She's the writer lady who's staying at the house,' Clementine explained to her friends.

'Well, that's lovely, isn't it? Not only do I get the pleasure of ferrying you all over the countryside, I'm not even mildly interesting enough to be considered,' Aunt Violet muttered under her breath.

'What did you say, Aunt Violet?' Clementine asked.

'I said I've told you, Clementine. I've never heard of Miss Richardson. Surely there's someone else in the family that you'd like to do your project on?' Her mouth tightened in a straight line.

Tilda saw Aunt Violet's face in the mirror then leaned over and whispered in Clementine's ear.

'Aunt *Violet*?' Clementine looked at her friend in confusion.

The old woman's ears perked up. 'Oh, Clementine, really, you'd like to do your project on me?'

Clementine still looked puzzled. 'No. You're not famous, Aunt Violet, and you haven't done anything interesting.'

'Well, for your information I've done plenty of interesting things, thank you very much. A lot more than that dowdy old woman upstairs.'

Aunt Violet's chin trembled and she looked as if she might cry.

Tilda watched her carefully in the mirror. 'Are you all right, Miss Appleby?'

'I'm fine, Tilda,' she snapped and stared at the road ahead. 'I know when I'm not wanted.'

Clementine bit her lip. 'I'm sorry, Aunt Violet.'

'Yes, I'm sorry too, Clementine,' the old woman said.

For the rest of the journey you could have heard a pin drop.

Uncle Digby was putting the rubbish out when Aunt Violet turned the car into the driveway and pulled up in front of the garage.

The children leapt out and ran around to collect their bags from the boot.

'Did you go to Pierre's?' the old man asked as Aunt Violet stalked past him.

'Yes, of course,' she huffed. 'Although no one in this family gives half a thought to my contributions.'

Uncle Digby frowned. He looked at Clementine. 'What was that all about?'

Clementine shrugged. 'I think Aunt Violet's upset because I didn't want to do my project on her.'

Uncle Digby's eyebrows shot up but all he said was, 'Oh, I see.' He retrieved the cake boxes. 'Why don't you go and play and I'll bring you something to eat soon.'

Clementine and the Hobbs children nodded and raced away inside to dump their bags.

'I'll get my ball,' said Clementine.

Soon the four of them were enjoying a

boisterous game of soccer on the back lawn. Lavender changed teams depending on the direction of the ball. The little pig squeaked and grunted as she wove in and out of legs, pushing the ball with her snout whenever it came her way. Pharaoh had joined in for a couple of minutes until a fluttery white butterfly stole his attention and he chased it into the hollyhocks instead.

'Hello Uncle Digby.' Clementine gave a wave as the old man appeared at the back door carrying a tray.

'Here's your afternoon tea at last,' he announced. 'Your mother and I have been caught up with guests.'

'Is Aunt Violet all right?' Clementine asked with a frown.

'I haven't seen her since you arrived home,' Uncle Digby said.

'Oh.' Clementine bit her lip and then shrugged and turned to her friends. 'Who wants some lemonade?'

Uncle Digby poured four tall glasses as the three siblings charged over.

Teddy downed his in one gulp. 'Ahhh!'

'Steady on there, Teddy, you'll give yourself a tummy ache.' Uncle Digby grinned at the lad, who reached for a chocolate brownie.

'Soccer makes you thirsty,' Teddy replied. 'And hungry.'

Lavender snuffled over to her water bowl by the back door.

'Your mother telephoned a little while ago and said that she and your father will be here in about fifteen minutes,' Uncle Digby informed the Hobbs children.

There was a groan all around.

'Come on, we'd better finish the game,' said Clementine. She put her glass down on the tray.

'Just leave all that and I'll get it later,' Uncle Digby said as he walked back to the door.

'Thanks, Uncle Digby,' the children chorused.

The old man smiled to himself.

'What's the score?' Tilda asked.

'It's one–nil, Clementine and Teddy's way,' Araminta announced.

'Come on, Mintie, we need to score a goal,' Tilda urged her big sister.

Clementine placed the ball in the middle of the lawn and ran backwards to stand beside Teddy. Teddy gave the referee's whistle and Araminta rushed forward. She kicked the ball as hard as she could down the pitch. Lavender looked up from where she was resting by the back steps, squealed and raced after it.

Teddy reached it first. 'Clementine,' he called as he kicked the ball past his big sister. Clementine stopped the ball and tried to dribble it past Tilda, who stole it back again and kicked it to Araminta.

'Come on, Tilda,' Araminta called as she raced towards the makeshift goal. She kicked and the ball flew past Clemmie and Teddy, straight into goal.

Tilda and Araminta raced towards each other, hands in the air, whooping and squealing. Lavender was squealing too.

'Good goal, Mintie,' Teddy called as he

picked up the ball and ran back to the centre of the lawn. 'It's one-all.'

The children regrouped. Tilda whistled and Teddy kicked the ball back towards Clementine. She raced down the pitch past Araminta and Tilda. Clementine looked at the goal, a frown of determination on her face. Araminta tackled Clementine just as the younger girl was about to kick for goal. They both connected with the ball at the same time. It flew into the air, higher and higher.

'Oh no!' Clementine shouted as she watched it soaring towards the house.

Smash! The ball splintered the window, leaving a gaping hole in the middle of the pane.

The Hobbs children clutched their hands to their mouths and stood still, waiting for someone to appear.

Araminta raced towards the house and peered up at the shattered glass. 'I'm sorry, Clemmie. That was all my fault.'

Clementine shook her head. 'No, it wasn't. I kicked it too.'

'Which window is it?' Teddy asked. He was trying to remember what was on the second floor.

Clementine looked up again and gasped. 'It's the Rose Room. That's where Miss Richardson is staying.'

'Is that the writer lady you talked about in the car?'

Clementine nodded. She wondered if the woman was sitting beneath the window at the desk. If she was she might have been injured by the glass. So far there was no screaming, nor an angry face appearing at the window.

'I have to tell Mummy,' said Clementine. She ran inside, leaving the Hobbs children in the garden wondering if there was anything they could do.

Clementine rushed into the kitchen. The room was empty.

She could hear voices in the hallway and poked her head around the door. Her mother was talking to a tall man carrying a suitcase and a woman with red hair.

Clementine wondered if Uncle Digby was upstairs. She closed the door and was about to go up the back stairs when the door swung towards her and Aunt Violet walked in.

'Hello Clementine.'

'Have you seen Uncle Digby?' the child asked urgently.

'Yes, and hello to you too,' the old woman said snarkily. 'He's upstairs sorting out some sort of drama.'

Clementine's tummy fluttered. She wondered if Miss Richardson was very upset about the window.

'What's the matter with you? You look as if you've seen a ghost,' said Aunt Violet.

Clementine shook her head. She didn't want to tell her great-aunt.

'I know when something is wrong, Clementine, despite the fact that you think I'm utterly useless. Where are the Hobbs children?'

'Outside,' Clementine said.

'Well, why are you in here?' Aunt Violet was like a terrier with a bone.

'I . . . I . . . had an accident,' Clementine blurted.

'Godfathers, Clementine, at your age! Too much excitement and running about,' Aunt Violet tutted and looked the girl up and down.

Clementine stared at her great-aunt quizzically.

'Come along and we'll get you some fresh clothes,' the woman said.

Clementine's mouth dropped open. 'Oh no, not that sort of accident, Aunt Violet. I'm not a baby.'

'No?' Aunt Violet arched her eyebrow. 'What sort of accident are you talking about?'

'I kicked the ball and it flew up really high and I didn't think I could even kick it that hard and –'

'Hello?' a voice called from the back door.

'Ana, darling, we're in here,' Aunt Violet answered.

Ana Hobbs stepped into the kitchen. Aunt Violet strode over to greet her with a kiss on both cheeks.

'Hello Clemmie, the children said that you were inside,' Ana said warmly.

'Hi,' Clementine said sheepishly. She wondered what else the children had told their mother.

'I just came to say thank you, Violet. No need to get Clarissa. I gather from the cars in the driveway that you must be busy tonight,' Ana said with a nod.

Aunt Violet's lip curled. 'Yes, unfortunately.'

'But it's wonderful for business,' Ana said, looking puzzled. 'I won't keep you. Are those the children's schoolbags over there?'

Clementine went to the sideboard and heaved the three bags over to Ana. The trio headed outside where Tilda, Teddy and Araminta were waiting.

'Say thank you,' Ana directed her children.

The twins and Araminta frowned at Clementine, wondering if she'd told her great-aunt about the window yet. 'Thanks,' they chorused.

'Sorry about the . . . you know,' said Araminta.

Aunt Violet frowned. 'What's that, Araminta?'

'Nothing, Aunt Violet,' Clementine said, shaking her head.

'Can Clementine come and play tomorrow, Mummy?' Tilda asked.

'Perhaps on Sunday, darling. Tomorrow we have to go and see Granny.'

'Don't forget we have to choose our famous friend too,' Teddy said.

'What's that?' Ana asked.

'We've got a project,' Tilda explained, 'and I'm going to do it on you, Mummy.'

'Oh, I can't wait to hear all about that.' Ana pretended to grimace and then turned to Aunt Violet.

'At least your children hold you in some regard,' Aunt Violet said, glaring at Clementine.

Ana frowned, wondering if there was a problem. 'Please thank Clarissa for having the children and say I'll give her a call on Sunday. Come along, kids, your father's in the car.'

The children and their mother gave a wave and disappeared around the side of the house.

Aunt Violet arched her eyebrow. 'Now, you'd better tell me about this accident, young lady.'

Clementine pointed upwards. 'I broke the window.'

'Oh, good heavens,' Aunt Violet began. Clementine cowered, waiting for her great-aunt to explode like a firecracker. Aunt Violet saw the girl's anxious face and her own expression softened. 'Is that all?'

Clementine was about to put her fingers in her ears when she realised what Aunt Violet had said. 'Aren't you mad at me?'

'Why would I be?' the old woman asked. 'It's nothing that can't be fixed.'

Clementine could hardly believe it. 'Are you all right, Aunt Violet?'

'No one was hurt, were they? You didn't hear any shouting from up in the room? It's just a pane of glass and it can be replaced,' the woman replied. 'Besides, Clementine, I can't tell you the number of windows your grandfather and I broke over the years with our overly enthusiastic games of cricket. It's something I was very good at as a child. I even played for the county – not that you'd want to know about that.'

'But it's Miss Richardson's room,' said Clementine. She was wondering why Aunt Violet was talking about cricket.

'Jolly good. That will give the silly old bat a reason to get outside for a while. That room smells like old socks and mustard after having her holed up for the entire week. I need to get some newspaper, a dustpan and broom and a garbage bag. And I'd best check if any of the glass has fallen out here too.'

Clementine ran along the hedge under the window and pointed at a large shard resting on top.

'Come away from that, Clementine,' Aunt Violet called. 'I'll do the cleaning up. Why don't you find Lavender and Pharaoh and bring them inside. I'll pop in and get what I need.'

Clementine watched Aunt Violet stride through the kitchen door. She had thought her great-aunt would be really mad but she wasn't. Clementine wondered if something had happened to her, but she had no idea what it was.

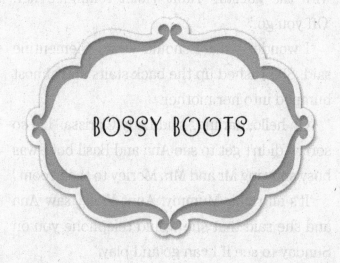

BOSSY BOOTS

'Right. Now to inspect the damage in the Rose Room,' said Aunt Violet as she wrapped up the shards of glass she'd found in the garden and put the bundle in the bin.

'May I come and help you?' Clementine asked.

'No, you need to run along and get changed,' Aunt Violet said.

'Why?' Clementine asked.

'Remember we're having that ghastly dinner

with the guests?' Aunt Violet reminded her. 'Off you go.'

'I wonder what I should wear,' Clementine said. She rushed up the back stairs and almost bumped into her mother.

'Oh hello, darling,' said Lady Clarissa. 'I'm so sorry I didn't get to see Ana and Basil but I was busy showing Mr and Mrs Morley to their room.'

'It's all right, Mummy. Aunt Violet saw Ana and she said that she would telephone you on Sunday to see if I can go and play.'

Aunt Violet bustled up behind Clementine. She was carrying an armful of newspaper and a dustpan and broom.

'Hello Aunt Violet,' said Clarissa. She eyed the goods in her hands. 'What are you doing with that?'

Clementine waited for her great-aunt to dob her in.

The old woman jutted her chin and said, 'Nothing for you to worry about at all.'

Lady Clarissa shook her head. 'What's got into you?'

'Can't a person indulge their passion for cleaning once in a while?'

'Aunt Violet, since when have you had a passion for cleaning?' Lady Clarissa asked, frowning.

'Well, now might be the one and only time you see it, so if I were you I'd keep quiet and get out of my way,' Aunt Violet announced and walked past.

'Don't let me stop you,' Clarissa called after her. 'Remember, dinner's at seven.'

'Quite right,' said Aunt Violet. 'Set an extra place at the table.'

'An extra place?' asked Lady Clarissa.

'Yes, Miss Richardson will be joining us.'

'I don't think so,' Lady Clarissa said slowly. 'I asked her this morning and she said that she was perfectly happy to have dinner in her room, as usual.'

'Well, I'm telling you she's having dinner downstairs whether she likes it or not.' Aunt Violet turned and disappeared along the hallway.

72

'Do you know what that was all about?' Lady Clarissa asked Clementine.

The child nodded and was about to tell her mother what had happened to the window when her great-aunt's sharp voice sounded from the end of the corridor. 'Clementine, run along and get dressed. You'd better make sure that Pharaoh and Lavender have had their dinner too.'

'Sorry, Mummy, I've got to go.' Clementine inched past her mother and made a dash for the top floor.

'I've put out a couple of dresses for you to choose from,' her mother called after her. 'They're hanging on the wardrobe door.'

Lady Clarissa walked down the back stairs, wondering what on earth was going on.

Violet Appleby knocked sharply on the door of the Rose Room.

'Yes,' a soft voice called from the other side. 'Come in.'

Aunt Violet poked her head around. 'Good heavens, what happened in here? Cyclone in a paper factory?'

The room was covered in paper from the floor to the bed and just about every surface in between.

'May I help you?' Miss Richardson rose from her seat at the small dining table in the corner. Already small and thin, she seemed even smaller and thinner after spending almost a week in her room. Her ice-grey hair was pulled back at the nape of her neck and she wore a grey cardigan and black slacks with a white shirt.

'I need to clear away some glass,' Aunt Violet said, giving the woman a cursory glance. 'And you need some sunlight.'

Miss Richardson frowned. 'I don't understand.'

'You must have heard it shatter,' said Aunt Violet. 'You haven't left the room, have you?'

'No, but I don't know what you're talking about.'

74

Violet Appleby picked her way through the paper maze on the floor, careful not to tread on any of the pages. She walked to the desk under the window, which was sprinkled with slivers of glass.

Miss Richardson followed her. 'Oh dear, how did that happen?' she gasped. 'I thought I heard a tinkling noise when I was in the bathroom.'

'One usually hears a tinkling noise in the bathroom.' Aunt Violet smiled at her own joke. 'But this one could be hazardous to your health.'

'Let me clear away some of those papers,' the old woman offered. 'I suppose it was fortunate I wasn't sitting there.'

'No, it's fine. I've got a better idea. I've arranged for someone to patch the window this evening. You'll have to come down and join us for dinner in the dining room,' Aunt Violet instructed. She hadn't yet made the call but Miss Richardson didn't need to know that.

'But I'd rather not,' Miss Richardson said. 'I'm working.'

'Yes, and I'd rather not have to eat dinner in the dining room with the guests but I don't have any choice in the matter. It's beautiful outside at the moment. Why don't you go for a walk around the garden? You could do with some colour, or we'll have the other guests thinking there's a vampire in residence.'

Miss Richardson's jaw dropped. 'Do you always boss your guests around in such a dreadful way?'

'Only if they need it,' huffed Aunt Violet. 'I don't know what you're working on but all this being cooped up can't be good for you. And it's not as if you're going to win a Nobel Prize, now, is it? Not for –' Aunt Violet picked up one of the pages and scanned the words – 'a book on the history of tractors? Godfathers, I'd be asleep after the first sentence. Off you go. I'll clear away the glass and the man can come and fix the window while you're at dinner.'

Miss Richardson wasn't used to being spoken to that way at all, but it was clear Violet Appleby was not to be trifled with.

'Do I need to change for dinner?' Miss Richardson asked.

Aunt Violet looked at her. 'No, you'll do. Perhaps you could brighten yourself up with a scarf or that brooch there.' Aunt Violet pointed at a sparkly pin on the dressing table.

Miss Richardson tied the scarf around her neck and stood near the door. She didn't know exactly what she was waiting for but she lingered nonetheless.

'Well, go on.' Aunt Violet shooed her away and went back to the smashed window.

Miss Richardson turned and walked out the door.

DINNER

Just before seven o'clock the guests gathered in the downstairs sitting room. Uncle Digby offered pre-dinner drinks while Lady Clarissa was busy in the kitchen. Mrs Mogg was there too, helping to prepare the meal. Entrees of salad and cold meats were already in place around the dining room table but the main course of roast beef, baked potatoes and a variety of vegetables was still simmering and sizzling in the ovens and on the cooktop.

'Clarissa, why don't you go and join everyone?' Mrs Mogg urged. 'Digby and I have this under control.'

'Thank you, Margaret,' Lady Clarissa said. She removed her apron and hung it on the hook beside the stove. 'You're a gem. Have you seen Clementine?'

At that moment the child skipped down the back stairs.

'Hello Mummy, hello Mrs Mogg.'

Mrs Mogg spun around. 'Oh my goodness, don't you look lovely?'

Clementine wore a pink dress sprinkled with a pretty rose pattern. It was tied at the back with a large green bow. She had a matching bow in her hair and silver ballet slippers on her feet. She gave a twirl. 'I love this dress. Thank you for making it, Mrs Mogg.'

'Come along, darling,' Lady Clarissa said. 'And what do you have to remember?'

'My best manners.' Clementine emphasised the word 'best'.

Lady Clarissa nodded. 'And?'

Clementine's nose wrinkled as she thought for a moment. 'Don't say anything mean about the guests.' She was remembering the time she told a lady her job sounded boring and her mother had got cross.

Lady Clarissa smiled. 'Yes, but I hope you never say mean things, Clementine.'

'Not on purpose,' the child replied.

Lady Clarissa led Clementine into the sitting room. Six guests were standing about drinking champagne and chatting. She scanned the room but there was no sign of Aunt Violet. A few minutes earlier Clarissa had heard her on the telephone making arrangements to fix something. But when she'd asked what it was, Aunt Violet had told her to mind her own business.

Clarissa introduced Clementine to Mr and Mrs Morley. He was a stocky man with thinning grey hair, while his wife was much taller with vivid red hair. Clementine thought they looked quite old, like Aunt Violet.

Mrs Morley leaned down, her long nose

almost touching Clementine's. 'Hello dear. Is it lovely to live in this great big old house?'

The child reeled backwards as the fishy cloud of Mrs Morley's breath hit her nostrils.

Clementine clamped her mouth shut and nodded her head like a trained seal. She could feel her face getting redder and her lungs growing tighter.

Mrs Morley frowned and wondered if there was something wrong with the girl. Perhaps she needed the toilet.

'Clementine, come and meet the Lees,' said Clarissa and guided her away.

The girl let out a huge sigh.

Mr Lee was a tall man with sleek black hair and round glasses. He wore a maroon-coloured velvet sports coat. His wife was blonde and wore a fitted dress patterned with sprays of white gardenias.

'Hello,' said Clementine. 'I like your jacket, Mr Lee. And Mrs Lee, your dress is lovely.'

'Oh, aren't you a darling?' Mrs Lee leaned down and met Clementine's gaze.

'And you smell nice too.' Clementine inhaled the woman's musk perfume, banishing the memory of Mrs Morley's tuna breath.

'What a precious child.' Mr Lee looked at his wife and they both giggled.

Mrs Lee touched her husband's arm. 'Maybe we should have one.'

Clementine shook her head slowly. 'Not all children are lovely, you know. There's a boy in my class called Joshua and his mother told Mummy that she'd like to give him away. So, you could have him, but you might not like him very much.'

The Lees giggled again.

Lady Clarissa wondered if she should have Uncle Digby clear away the extra place setting for Miss Richardson. There was no sign of the woman, or Aunt Violet for that matter.

The sound of a distant gong interrupted the chatter.

'They're ready for us in the dining room,' Lady Clarissa announced.

'Do you always use the gong?' asked a round

woman in a fluttery posh voice. She wore a shimmery jacket and a pillbox hat with a tiny veil covering her eyes. An enormous silver handbag hung over her shoulder. Clementine thought she could turn it upside down and use it as a cubbyhouse.

'No, Mrs Biggins, not these days. The house was run much more formally when I was little, especially if grandmamma was here visiting,' Lady Clarissa explained. 'Now if you'd like to follow me . . .'

Lady Clarissa walked into the foyer and across to the dining room. The guests paraded behind her. Clementine stayed at the back, showing everyone her best manners and letting them go first.

The group disappeared through the dining room door just as Aunt Violet walked down the main staircase. She was wearing a lovely cream silk pants-suit. A short, grey-haired woman was beside her.

'Hello Aunt Violet,' Clementine said. 'Is everything all right?'

'Yes, except that I must look a terrible mess. I only had a minute to get changed because I've been busy sorting out someone's problems.'

'Oh,' Clementine said with a gulp. She wondered how long it would be until her mother learned of the broken window. 'Is it fixed?'

'I just let the glazier in the back door. And don't worry. Clementine, I'm not planning on telling your mother. I'm sure she has enough to worry about.' Aunt Violet gestured towards the woman beside her. 'This is Miss Richardson.'

'Thank you, Aunt Violet. Hello Miss Richardson,' Clementine said. 'I'm sorry about your window. I didn't mean to break it. The ball just kept going and going and *smash!*'

Miss Richardson looked at Clementine but remained tight-lipped.

'And I'm sorry I came to your room the other night. I just wanted to help,' Clementine babbled.

Miss Richardson lowered her eyes to the floor. 'Never mind.'

'It's all right,' Clementine said. 'I know lots of grown-ups don't like children. Aunt Violet doesn't, do you?'

'Don't be ridiculous, Clementine,' her great-aunt retorted. 'I like some children. Just not the snivelling ones. Which is most of them.'

Clementine grinned.

Aunt Violet walked into the dining room followed by Miss Richardson and Clementine.

The rest of the guests were taking their seats around the table. Each guest's place was marked with a small card bearing their name in fancy script.

Miss Richardson was seated to Lady Clarissa's left, opposite Clementine.

Mrs Biggins sat beside Miss Richardson. Her husband was even larger than she was and spilled out over the sides of his chair. He had a black moustache and wild hair. Clementine thought he looked like a cartoon character, with his bulging cheeks and dimpled chin.

Uncle Digby appeared. He began to take the napkins from the bread-and-butter plates and shake them into the guests' laps. When he reached Mrs Biggins, he noticed the woman was still clutching her handbag.

'Would you like me to take that for you, ma'am?' Uncle Digby asked. 'I can put it somewhere safe.'

'No, don't touch!' Mrs Biggins snapped and gripped the handles tighter.

'Very well.' He raised his eyebrows playfully at Clementine. She put her hands over her mouth to stop a giggle from escaping.

Mrs Biggins pushed the bag onto her knees and Uncle Digby shook her napkin out and laid it over the top. It looked like a circus tent on her lap.

When Uncle Digby reached Clementine, he leaned down and whispered in the child's ear.

'What do you think she has in that bag, eh?'

Clementine put her hands on either side of his ear and whispered, 'Gold. Maybe diamonds too.'

Uncle Digby winked. 'I'll try again later so we can take a peek.'

Lady Clarissa smiled at her guests as she leaned ever so slightly towards Clementine. 'What are you two up to?' she murmured.

'It's a secret.' Clementine put her finger on her lip. Her mother shook her head a little and smiled.

SURPRISE!

'Good evening, ladies and gentlemen,' Lady Clarissa said from her seat at the head of the table. 'Before we start, I'd like to introduce everyone, if I may?'

Aunt Violet rolled her eyes and muttered, 'What is this? A self-help group?'

Lady Clarissa eyeballed her aunt and continued. 'I think all of you have met my daughter, Clementine Rose, and that's my aunt, Miss Appleby.' She nodded at the old woman opposite her, then turned to her left. 'This is Miss Richardson and next to her we have Mrs Biggins, then Mr Biggins and Mrs Morley. Across the table is Mr Morley and on my right we have Mr and Mrs Lee. Bon appétit.'

The group nodded politely at one another and picked up their cutlery. A few minutes later, Mr Morley asked, 'So, what brings everyone to Penberthy Floss?'

'We love a country weekend,' Mr Biggins said. He smiled at his wife, but she was too preoccupied with her handbag to notice.

'It's our first wedding anniversary.' Mrs Lee fluttered her eyelashes and patted her husband's arm.

'Oh, congratulations . . . Well done . . .' a chorus of voices said at once.

'What about you, Mr Morley?' Aunt Violet asked.

'I'm writing a book, actually. I thought it would be nice to find a peaceful place in the country to work on it,' the man said with a smug smile.

Aunt Violet groaned and then tried to

hide it by saying, 'What a coincidence. Miss Richardson is also writing a book.' She raised her eyebrows at the woman. Miss Richardson focused on the lettuce leaves in front of her while her cheeks grew red.

'Oh really, Miss Richardson. Is that so? What do you write?' Mr Morley asked.

She glanced up. 'It's nothing, Mr Morley. Just a little project.'

'Well, not everyone's as talented as my Dennis,' declared Mrs Morley. She grinned and revealed a set of teeth as yellow as cheese. 'But you mustn't give up, dear. If you stick with it and perhaps join some writers' groups, you never know what might happen. Although at your age you really mustn't leave it too long.'

Miss Richardson frowned and a squeak escaped from her lips. Clementine watched her closely from the other side of the table.

Digby Pertwhistle entered and cleared the entree plates.

'And what is it that *you've* written, Mr Morley?' Miss Richardson asked.

'Dennis has done a lovely little book for kiddies,' his wife answered for him. 'It's about a train and a dragon and there are some fairies too.'

Clementine's eyes lit up. 'Are you famous, Mr Morley?'

'Clemmie,' Lady Clarissa whispered and frowned at the child. 'Manners, darling.'

'Sorry, Mummy. It's just that I have to do a school project about a famous person and I wondered if Mr Morley was famous.'

'Well, I don't like to boast but I did just have a lovely spread in our village newspaper,' the man replied.

Mrs Mogg and Uncle Digby arrived bearing the main course as Miss Richardson coughed delicately into her napkin.

'Where can we buy this book of yours, Morley?' Mr Biggins asked as Mrs Mogg set a plate of roast beef and vegetables in front of him.

Mrs Morley answered for him again. 'Well, it's not quite ready yet and we're just waiting to hear back from a publisher, but they're very excited about it. I'm sure they're going to take it on.'

A 'huh' sound blurted from Miss Richardson's lips. She took a mouthful of food and chewed it rapidly.

'Your project sounds exciting, Clementine,' Mrs Lee said from the other end of the table. 'Who else do you think you might choose for it?'

'I'm not sure,' Clementine said, her brow furrowing. The question had been in the back of her mind all afternoon. 'I thought about Tilda and Teddy's mum, Ana, because she was a famous ballerina. But Tilda is going to talk about her and it would be silly to have two projects on the same person.'

'What about a singer?' Mr Lee suggested.

'No, the child doesn't want popular non-sense,' Mr Biggins tutted. 'She should be studying a prime minister or an explorer.'

Aunt Violet rolled her eyes. 'Well, that sounds frightfully dull.'

It seemed that almost everyone around the table had an opinion about Clementine's project.

Digby Pertwhistle stepped forward to top up Clementine's water glass. 'What about your favourite author? The one who writes all those poems and stories we like,' he whispered.

Clementine's eyes lit up. 'That's a great idea, Uncle Digby.'

The others continued their chatter until Clementine announced, 'I've decided.'

The hubbub died down.

Just as she was about to speak, Clementine noticed Mrs Biggins's napkin moving. It seemed to flutter upwards.

Clementine leaned forward and tilted her head as far as she could to see over the table.

Mrs Biggins jabbed a piece of meat with her fork. But instead of lifting it to her mouth, she put it in her lap.

The napkin moved again.

'Excuse me, Mrs Biggins, but why are you feeding your napkin?' Clementine asked.

Eight pairs of eyes suddenly turned towards Mrs Biggins, who hastily set her fork on her plate.

'What are you talking about?' she snapped, then shovelled some more food onto her fork and gobbled it down.

But Clementine wasn't convinced and neither was Miss Richardson, who jumped when the napkin wriggled again. 'Mrs Biggins, is something in your bag?'

Mrs Biggins frowned and smoothed the napkin on her lap. Just as she did, a fluffy white head poked out.

'Oh my heavens, what's that?' Aunt Violet shrieked.

Miss Richardson giggled. 'You're very cute!'

Clementine giggled too.

'What are you laughing at? It's not funny at all!' Aunt Violet cried.

The tiny creature pushed itself forward and stole a piece of roast beef from Miss Richardson's plate. The old woman's eyes lit up. 'Cheeky!'

'Get it out of here!' Aunt Violet demanded.

Mrs Biggins grasped at the animal but the little dog leapt from her lap onto the table. It danced down the centre, knocking the candelabra into a flaming wobble, which Uncle Digby somehow managed to catch. Arms reached out from all over the place to stop the escapee.

'Polly! Come back!' Mrs Biggins shouted.

'I'll get her.' Clementine took off after the powder puff, which was half the size of Lavender.

Polly ran towards Aunt Violet, who dived left and then right trying to block the creature's path. 'You're not going anywhere, mutt,' Aunt Violet yelled.

But Polly had other ideas. She ran straight through the middle of Aunt Violet's plate, leaving paw prints in the gravy, and jumped onto the woman's lap and down to the floor.

'Urgh, my suit! It's ruined!' Aunt Violet stared in horror at the brown stains on her cream outfit.

By now the entire party was on their feet, set for the chase.

Mrs Mogg was coming to check on the progress of dinner when Polly raced through the woman's legs and down the hallway. The little dog left yet more gravy splodges in her wake.

'Polly!' Clementine called and raced after her. The rest of the group were hot on her heels.

'Oh, my darling doggy,' Mrs Biggins wailed. 'Don't you hurt her!'

'That's not a dog. It's a polishing cloth with legs,' Aunt Violet squawked.

'How dare you?' Mrs Biggins gasped.

'And how dare you bring a dog to dinner? I'm sure Clarissa told you that we don't take pets. Heavens knows how much they'd upset Pharaoh – and Lavender, for that matter.'

Clementine saw the creature disappear through the swinging kitchen door and ran after her. Finally Polly stopped by the cooker, trapped between Pharaoh and

Lavender, who hissed and grunted at their unexpected visitor.

'Polly,' Clementine called in a singsong voice. 'Here Polly, would you like something to eat?' Clementine spotted some leftover beef on a plate on the table. She grabbed a small piece and offered it to the dog.

By now the entire dinner party was standing behind the child, craning their necks to see the tiny pup.

'What is it?' Mrs Lee asked.

'It's a Teacup Pomeranian,' Mrs Biggins said. 'But what on earth is that?' She pointed at the sphynx cat.

'That's my Pharaoh and you'd better hope he doesn't take a dislike to Polly or things might get ugly,' said Aunt Violet.

Polly sniffed the air as Clementine slowly walked towards her. Pharaoh yowled.

'You can have some too,' the child said. She tore the tasty morsel in half and offered a piece in each hand. Pharaoh slunk forward and took the meat before retreating to Lavender's basket.

Lavender watched the little dog, whose tail swished like a windscreen wiper on high speed.

Polly took two steps forward then danced back. She wriggled and waggled her tail and eventually snatched the piece of meat from Clementine's hand. Clementine reached out and picked the little fur ball up, clutching her to her chest.

'Give her to me!' Mrs Biggins demanded.

Clementine stroked the top of the dog's head. 'You're so cute,' she cooed.

Mrs Biggins snatched the dog from Clementine's arms.

'Well, I think we should be getting back to dinner,' Lady Clarissa said loudly, hoping that the adventure hadn't caused her other guests too much distress. The last thing Penberthy House needed was a bad review.

'That dog's not welcome!' Aunt Violet sniffed.

'Come along, Muriel,' Mr Biggins blustered. 'We'll get our things.'

'Yes, and I'll be sending you a bill for my

dry-cleaning too.' Aunt Violet spun around and stalked away.

Most of the group retreated to the dining room, leaving Clementine and her mother with the Bigginses.

'There's no need for you to leave,' Lady Clarissa said calmly. 'We don't usually accommodate pets but it's getting late and there are no other hotels close by. Why don't we get one of Lavender's spare baskets and a water bowl and some food, and Polly can spend the rest of the evening in your room.'

'That's very kind, Lady Clarissa,' said Mr Biggins. He glared at his wife. 'Isn't it?'

'Yes,' the woman whispered.

'I told you we should have left her with your sister but oh no, why would you listen to me,' Mr Biggins hissed through gritted teeth.

'Clemmie, run along to the dining room and let Uncle Digby know we'll be ready for dessert in ten minutes,' Lady Clarissa instructed.

Clementine nodded and scampered away.

STORIES

ortunately, no one else seemed terribly offended by Polly the Pomeranian. The guests were all chattering happily when Lady Clarissa returned with Mr and Mrs Biggins in tow.

'I thought you were leaving,' Aunt Violet sniped.

'No, your niece has kindly allowed us to stay. Polly's in our room,' the man said. 'She won't be bothering you again.'

'Clarissa, we have rules about pets,' Aunt

Violet began. 'And this suit will not clean itself.'

Lady Clarissa ignored her aunt and walked to the other end of the dining room.

'I'm happy to pay for your dry-cleaning, Miss Appleby,' Mr Biggins offered.

'Oh, yes you . . . Oh. Right. Just as well, then.' Aunt Violet pulled a face and took a large gulp from the glass in front of her.

Clementine was watching Miss Richardson, who was quietly watching everyone else around the table. She looked serious again but Clementine remembered that she'd laughed when Polly popped up. Maybe she wasn't as cranky as Clementine had first thought. She could have one of those faces that looked cross even when she didn't mean to.

'I thought Polly was funny too, Miss Richardson,' Clementine said to the woman. 'It was just like a story Uncle Digby read with me last week. It was about a naughty dog who wriggled into the next door neighbour's house through the cat door and ate everything, including the father's socks.'

Miss Richardson frowned. 'Did you like that story?'

Clementine nodded. 'I loved it. It was *Melville the Mangy Mutt* by Agnes Wells. She's my favourite writer in the whole world. That's who I'm going to do my project on. I was about to say that when Polly escaped.'

A deep row of frown lines furrowed Miss Richardson's brow. 'I thought children didn't like her books any more.'

Clementine shook her head. 'I love them.'

'Well.' A strange smile settled on the woman's lips. 'That is a surprise.'

'Do you know her?' Clementine asked.

'I did a long time ago,' Miss Richardson replied.

Mrs Lee smiled. 'I loved her books when I was a little girl too, Clementine. They were old-fashioned romps even –'

Mrs Morley interrupted her. 'I've heard she's a crotchety old thing. Doesn't like children at all. Imagine that! Not like my Dennis. He adores children and they adore him.'

'Who told you that?' Miss Richardson asked.

'There was that article about her in the newspaper recently. The journalist said that her books were dull and old-fashioned and showed no love of children at all. If I were her I'd retire to the seaside and forget about writing another thing.'

Miss Richardson's face fell. 'You shouldn't always believe everything you read, Mrs Morley.'

Clementine's eyes were wide. 'Could you help me with my project, Miss Richardson?'

Lady Clarissa had been listening to the conversation too. 'Clementine, Miss Richardson doesn't have time for that. She's very busy working on her book.'

Miss Richardson didn't say a word. She simply focused on the passionfruit cheesecake that Uncle Digby had just put down in front of her.

'Oh well, Mr Smee will help me,' Clementine said. 'And Uncle Digby.'

Digby Pertwhistle gave the girl a wink.

PROJECTS

The rest of the weekend whizzed by. Apart from Miss Richardson, all the guests were gone by midday on Sunday. Clementine was disappointed not to see Polly again but Mr and Mrs Biggins had left first thing on Saturday morning. Mr Biggins was true to his word and left an envelope with a rather large sum of money to pay for Aunt Violet's dry-cleaning. On Sunday Ana had telephoned to invite Clementine around. She had spent the day with the Hobbs children, exploring their garden by the stream and playing in the newly built tree house.

On Monday morning, twenty pairs of eager eyes greeted their teacher in the Year One classroom. 'Good morning, Mr Smee,' the children chorused.

Clementine thought he looked especially handsome today with his red polka-dot tie.

'Did everyone have a chance to think about their Famous Friend project over the weekend?' the teacher asked.

The children nodded.

'Well, I'm keen to know who you've chosen.' Mr Smee pointed to Angus. 'Who's your famous friend?'

'I'm doing Hedley Humphrey,' said Angus. 'He was a famous mountain climber.'

The teacher nodded. 'Good choice. Have you thought about what you're going to wear?'

Angus's eyes lit up. 'Yup. I've already got some ropes too, and Dad said that I could borrow a pickaxe but I'm the only one allowed to touch it.'

Mr Smee frowned. He'd speak to Angus's dad about that. 'What about you, Clementine?'

'I'm going to be Agnes Wells,' the child replied.

'I loved her books when I was a little boy but I didn't know kids still read them today. I think she's gone out of fashion, although I don't know why. Maybe we could read one of her books together in class.'

Clementine nodded. 'That's a great idea. But I don't know anything about her apart from her books. Can you help me find out some more things about her, Mr Smee?'

'Sure can, Clemmie. We'll do that this afternoon. Miss Critchley is going to help us too.'

The morning sped past. Mr Smee led the children through all sorts of reading, writing and mathematics activities. After morning tea there was singing and craft. Finally, after lunch, the children met Mr Smee and Miss Critchley outside the library.

The head teacher was very impressed with

the famous friends the students had chosen, apart from Joshua's pick. Once she and Mr Smee convinced him that Batman wasn't a real person, it was time to get down to work. Tilda's job was easy because she was doing her project on her mother. But Mr Smee said that she still had to write her talk and work out how she was going to present it to the group. Tilda was planning to give the audience a short ballet lesson.

'Where can we find out about Miss Wells?' Clementine asked Mr Smee.

'Sometimes there are facts about authors at the back of their books,' he said. 'And why don't we type her name into the computer and see what comes up?'

Clementine flipped to the back cover of the book she'd found on the shelf. There was a black-and-white photograph of a serious-looking young woman. Her hair was pulled back and she wore glasses on the tip of her nose. Pinned to her lapel was a sparkly brooch in the shape of a heart.

Clementine began to read the words aloud, sounding out the hard ones she didn't know. 'It says that Miss Wells has written lots of books and she lives in the city.'

'Mmm.' Mr Smee scratched his chin. 'I've just printed something off for you, but I'm afraid it doesn't tell us much. Miss Wells seems to be a very private person.'

'Could I just say a few things about her and then recite one of her poems for my presentation?' Clementine asked.

'That's a great idea,' Mr Smee agreed. 'You only have a minute or two anyway, or the assembly will go all afternoon.'

Mrs Bottomley's head appeared over the top of one of the bookshelves. 'Yes, and we wouldn't want that, would we Mr Smee?'

'Oh, hello Ethel,' he said.

'It's Mrs Bottomley, thank you,' the woman snapped. 'Next thing the children will be calling you Roderick. Jolly hippy.'

Mr Smee waggled his eyebrows at Clementine, who tried not to laugh.

'What are you doing over here anyway?' Mrs Bottomley demanded. 'I was planning to bring Kindergarten for story time.'

'I'm sorry, Mrs Bottomley,' said Mr Smee. 'I booked the library so that Year One could start their projects.'

'No, you didn't. I can't see your name anywhere on this list.'

'I think you'll find that's last week's sheet,' Mr Smee said.

Ethel Bottomley scanned the page. She squeezed her lips tightly. 'Oh. I'll just take a book back to class with me then.'

Before she left, Mrs Bottomley scribbled 'Kindergarten' into every afternoon slot for the rest of the week.

A POEM

Clementine stood in the middle of the front stairs, looking up at her grandparents' portraits. She was practising a poem for Friday's presentation, but something wouldn't stick. She recited the first verse then her mind went blank again.

'It's hopeless,' she said and stamped her foot.

Clementine hadn't noticed Miss Richardson standing on the landing. The woman had spent most of the week hidden in her room, but

Clementine had bumped into her in the garden a couple of times. On those occasions they'd talked a little, but whenever Clementine asked about Miss Wells, the woman made an excuse and scurried off as fast as her little legs would carry her.

Clementine started the poem from the beginning again. She stopped at exactly the same place.

'*And just as quick, you save the day, and make the bad things go away,*' a voice said from upstairs.

Clementine turned and saw the grey-haired woman. 'Oh, thank you, Miss Richardson. I don't know why I can't remember.'

'Why don't you think about the last word in each line because those are the ones that rhyme. That might help.'

'That's a great idea,' Clementine enthused. She recited the lines to her grandfather's portrait. 'Did you hear that Grandpa? I remembered. How do you know that poem?' She turned to look back at Miss Richardson

but the woman had gone. 'Thank you, Miss Richardson,' Clementine called, hoping that wherever she was she heard it.

'Who are you talking to?' Aunt Violet asked as she appeared on the landing above Clementine.

'Miss Richardson just helped me remember my poem. Do you want to hear it?'

'No, not especially,' said Aunt Violet as she stomped past. Clementine sighed loudly and her great-aunt turned around. 'It's not that I don't want to hear it, Clementine, it's just that I thought I'd save it until the performance at school.'

'Are you coming?' Clementine was surprised to hear it.

'I thought the invitation said that all members of the family were welcome,' the old woman remarked.

'It did,' said Clementine. 'But you don't usually like coming to my school things and I thought you were mad at me because I'm not doing my project on you.'

'All right then, fussy pants, I won't come,' Aunt Violet sniffed and strode across the foyer.

'But Aunt Violet, I want you to,' Clementine called after her.

The woman stopped. She spun around and stared up at the blonde-haired child. 'Do you mean that?'

Clementine nodded. 'Yes, of course I do.'

'I'll come then. But only because you begged me to.' Aunt Violet turned once more, opened the front door and disappeared outside.

Clementine was confused. 'Was she always so tricky, Grandpa?' She could have sworn she saw the old man nodding his head.

A LETTER

On Friday morning, Clementine rolled over and jolted awake. 'It's today!' She leapt out of bed and skipped across the hallway to the bathroom.

'Good morning, Aunt Violet,' she called to her great-aunt, who had just emerged from the Blue Room.

The old woman's hair looked like a bird's nest and her eyes were bleary. 'Godfathers, Clementine, keep your voice down. Some of us aren't as enthusiastic about the mornings as others.'

'You'd better get ready. We're all going to school together, remember?' Clementine said. She couldn't wait for the special assembly at nine o'clock.

'Yes, yes, that's why I'm about to have a shower,' Aunt Violet sighed and shuffled into the bathroom.

Clementine's uniform was hanging on the wardrobe door. But that's not what she was wearing today. The children had to come to school in costume and Mr Smee said they could stay in their special clothes all day. Clementine thought that would upset Mrs Bottomley a lot.

Pictures of Agnes Wells weren't easy to find. Clementine and Uncle Digby had searched and searched and there were only black-and-white photographs of her when she was young. Clementine and Mr Smee had worked out that she'd be almost eighty by now. In one picture Miss Wells wore a pintucked blouse and a flared skirt, with the same little sparkly heart brooch Clementine had seen in all the other photographs. Clementine decided to wear her pink blouse with the pintucks and peter pan collar. She teamed it with a green skirt of her mother's, which Mrs Mogg tucked and trimmed.

In the attic she and her mother had found a pair of Granny's old reading glasses and a pair of mid-heeled navy shoes. Uncle Digby punched the lenses out of the glasses and Clarissa helped Clementine stuff the shoes with paper so they'd fit. Best of all, her mother had found a brooch almost the same as the one in the pictures. It was a little bit bigger and had belonged to Clementine's grandmother. She was only allowed to wear it because the sparkly stones weren't real diamonds. She had a pile of Agnes Wells's books to carry and a notepad and pen too.

'Look at you!' Lady Clarissa giggled when she saw Clementine standing in front of her bedroom mirror.

'Hello Mummy, what do you think? Do I look like Miss Wells?'

Lady Clarissa nodded. 'Let's just get your hair up and then you'll be perfect, darling.' She grabbed the brush from Clementine's dressing table. A few minutes later she was done. 'I'd better hop in the shower. Why don't you go downstairs and have breakfast and then we can get going. Maybe it's best if you wear your ballet flats and put those other shoes on later. We don't want you taking a tumble on the stairs.'

Clementine agreed and slipped the navy shoes off. She popped them into her schoolbag and stuffed her feet into her favourite red ballet flats.

'I wish you could come with us, Lavender,' she said to the little pig, who was sitting in her basket. 'I'd love you to hear my poem.'

Lavender grunted.

As Clementine was on her way downstairs the doorbell rang. 'I'll get it!' she called.

Clementine opened the front door. A man in a blue postman's uniform was holding an envelope. 'Good morning, miss,' he said.

'Hello, may I help you?' Clementine asked.

'I have a letter for Miss Abigail Richardson,' the man replied.

Clementine smiled. 'I can take it up to her.'

'Thank you.' He gave Clementine a strange look and handed over the envelope.

'We're doing a special assembly at school this morning,' she said. 'I'm dressed up as an author. Her name is Agnes Wells and she's very old.'

'Oh.' The man rubbed his chin. 'Well, that explains the outfit. You know, I think I read her books when I was a little boy. Enjoy your assembly.'

Clementine nodded. 'I will.'

The man gave a wave as Clementine closed the front door and scurried upstairs.

She skipped down the hallway to the Rose Room and knocked sharply on the door. 'Excuse me, Miss Richardson.'

'Yes,' the woman called from within.

Clementine pushed open the door and walked through. Miss Richardson was standing by the window and looking out into the garden.

'I have a letter for you,' Clementine announced.

The old woman turned around. 'Oh my.' Miss Richardson looked Clementine up and down. 'Don't you look sweet.'

'It's for the assembly today. I'm Agnes Wells, remember?' Clementine said as she handed over the envelope. Miss Richardson looked at it and hesitated, then slid her finger under the flap. She unfolded the page and gasped.

'What's the matter?'

'It seems . . .' She hesitated. 'I've won an award.' Deep furrows creased her forehead.

'That's wonderful,' Clementine said. 'What's it for?'

'It's a lifetime achievement award from the Society of Children's Writers. But I didn't think anyone cared for my work any more . . .' The old woman's voice trailed off and her eyes glistened with tears.

'I thought you wrote history books,' Clementine said.

Miss Richardson wiped her eyes and nodded. 'Yes, that's why I came here, but I don't seem to be making much progress with that. When I heard you reciting that poem I started something else.'

'Ooh, what is it?' Clementine asked.

'Just a silly story about a cat and a pig,' Miss Richardson replied.

Clementine's eyes widened. 'We have a cat and a pig. Is it about Pharaoh and Lavender?'

But Miss Richardson wasn't listening. She was re-reading the letter, staring at the page.

Clementine looked at the papers on the desk. She didn't like to mind other people's business because her mummy said that was wrong, but she couldn't help noticing a book she loved sitting among the pages.

'That's a great story,' she said, pointing. 'Aunt Violet and I have been reading it at bedtime.'

Miss Richardson still seemed far away. Clementine studied the woman. She was wearing a lemon-coloured blouse and a blue skirt. But it was something else that caught the child's attention. 'Oh! That's funny.'

'What's the matter?' Miss Richardson asked, jolting back to the present.

Clementine pointed at the brooch on the woman's blouse. 'Look, it's just like mine.' Suddenly her mouth gaped open.

Miss Richardson smiled. 'Fancy that.'

Clementine looked at Miss Richardson and then at the book on the desk.

'You don't really write boring tractor history books at all, do you, Miss Richardson?' Clementine asked.

Miss Richardson shook her head.

Clementine jigged about excitedly. 'I think you write much more exciting things. Please, may I ask you something? It's very important.' Clementine could barely contain herself.

'Yes, of course,' the woman said.

Clementine took a step closer and told Miss Agnes Wells her grand plan.

SHOWTIME

lementine's stomach fluttered. The children in Year One were lined up across the stage, ready to give their presentations. There was a colourful mix of explorers and doctors, movie stars and singers. Tilda looked beautiful in a red tutu with her hair pulled back into a bun. Teddy was holding an old-fashioned movie camera and looked just like his father. He had round glasses perched on the tip of his nose and a beret on his head. Poppy was dressed up as Cleopatra, with a black wig, and Sophie wore a lab coat as she was the famous scientist Marie Curie.

'What's happened to alphabetical order?' Mrs Bottomley tutted from where she was sitting at the end of her Kindergarten row. 'I knew they'd be a disaster in no time.'

Mr Smee walked onto the stage and stood behind the microphone.

'Good morning, everyone,' he said.

'Go-ood mor=ning, Mr Sme-e,' the children chorused back.

'The students of Year One have really amazed me with their hard work and wonderful ideas. They're going to tell you all about their famous friends, who they've dressed up as today. Without any further ado, I welcome Astrid.'

Astrid walked to the microphone in the middle of the stage. She was dressed in a yellow ball gown with a tiara on her head, but she was carrying a riding whip and wearing boots.

'Good morning, loyal subjects.' She gave a funny wave and the audience giggled. 'My name is Queen Georgiana and I'd like to tell you about my life . . .'

At the end, she stepped to the side of the microphone and curtsied. The parents and children clapped loudly. Each child took their turn. Mr Smee stood close by in case he needed to help anyone with their reading. When Tilda spoke, she asked all of the children, teachers and parents to stand. She showed them how to practise first and second position, then twirl around. The audience thoroughly enjoyed themselves.

Clementine was last of all. She took a deep breath and looked out into the audience until she found where Aunt Violet, Uncle Digby and her mother were sitting.

'I'd like to tell you about my famous friend. She writes books and poems for children. She's written more than one hundred of them and children love them because they're funny and adventurous and they make you feel as if you could jump right in and be part of the action.

'My famous friend was born during the war,

so she's old now. She never got married and she doesn't have any children but in a way her books are like her children. And the last thing is that her real name is different to her writer name. I'm going to read you my favourite poem that she wrote.'

Clementine took a deep breath. '"Bitten by the Bug", by Agnes Wells . . .'

At the end of the recital, the parents and children clapped wildly. Clementine stood in the middle of the stage and took a bow. Then another.

She waited until the clapping had stopped and then looked to the left of the stage. Mr Smee nodded and stepped in front of the microphone.

'Ladies and gentlemen, boys and girls, I think Clementine has a surprise for us,' he said.

'Is it chocolate?' a Kindergarten lad called. Ethel Bottomley gave the boy one of her most evil stares.

'Is it a monkey?' another boy with wild black curls yelled.

The assembly hall erupted with laughter.

'That's stupid!' a girl in Kindergarten said.

'You're stu–' the monkey boy began to shout.

'Children, stop it now,' Ethel Bottomley hissed through her teeth.

Aunt Violet shook her head. 'Poor Ethel. Fancy having to put up with that nonsense every day.'

'All right, everyone, settle down,' said Mr Smee. 'What did you want to say, Clementine?'

Clementine stood up straight and loudly announced, 'I'd like you to meet someone.'

Miss Richardson walked across the stage and stood beside the girl.

'What's she doing up there?' Aunt Violet tutted. 'I did wonder why Clementine asked her to come.'

Uncle Digby and Lady Clarissa smiled at one another. Clementine had told them what was going on at home while they were waiting for Aunt Violet to finish getting ready.

'This is Miss Agnes Wells,' said Clementine. 'My famous friend.'

'I love her!' Joshua called from the stage.

A murmur of 'me too . . . she's cool . . . awesome . . .' raced around the room.

Miss Wells's cheeks blushed fiery red.

The parents at the back of the room stood up and clapped loudly.

'Thanks for all those great stories,' one of the fathers called out.

'Hear, hear!' Mrs Bottomley echoed.

Mr Smee looked out and was stunned to see the Kindergarten teacher on her feet and clapping louder than everyone else. He smiled at her and Mrs Bottomley gave him the smallest hint of a nod. Mr Smee couldn't believe it.

'See, Miss Wells?' Clementine reached out to hold the woman's hand. 'It's not true what Mrs Morley said. Everyone loves you.'

Miss Richardson beamed at the audience. 'Thank you, Clementine,' she whispered. 'Thank you.'

Bitten by the Bug

One morning snuggled in my bed
A little bug appeared and said,
'I see that you have learned a lot
Since you were just a tiny tot.
You crawled, then walked and now you run
It's time for you to have more fun.
I have so many friends to share:
Three bears and a girl with curly hair;
A crazy fellow called McGee,
Who has a fight with biting fleas;
There's Charlie making sweets galore;
Wild things on boats and so much more.

'Hurry up and take a look
Inside this lovely picture book.
You can travel far and wide,
If you pretend it's you inside.
I know it really is bizarre,
How at your age you can drive a car,
Or fight a monster, or save a life,

You can get yourself in lots of strife.
And just as quick, you save the day
And make the bad things go away.
There are tales about most anything
To make you laugh and cry and sing.'

I told the bug that I'm too small
I won't read books until I'm tall
He shook his head and frowned at me.
'That's just not true – you wait and see.
We'll learn together from today
And next thing you'll be on your way.'

I told the bug I'd try my best
In this love-of-reading quest.
I opened up a storybook
And crawled inside to take a look.
Suddenly I was right there,
Creeping down the little stairs.
There was a wolf outside the door,
He opened up his mouth to roar.
I scrambled up the chimney stack
Jumped off the roof and out the back,

Racing through a forest tall,
Such an adventure for one so small

The little bug climbed off my bed,
And with a smile he softly said,
'I think my job here is now done,
I've opened up a world of fun.
I'm sure that it has been quite painless,
To ignore me would be simply brainless.
You're hooked and now I'm on my way
To find another kid who'll play.
You've been bitten, that's for sure,
The book bug will be back for more.
Just remember what I said
There is so much yet to be read.'

The clever bug went on his way
And now I'm reading every day
He's right, you know, I'm on the hook
There's nothing better than a book!

CAST OF CHARACTERS

The Appleby household

Clementine Rose Appleby — Five-year-old daughter of Lady Clarissa

Lavender — Clemmie's teacup pig

Lady Clarissa Appleby — Clementine's mother and the owner of Penberthy House

Digby Pertwhistle — Butler at Penberthy House

| Aunt Violet Appleby | Clementine's grandfather's sister |
| Pharaoh | Aunt Violet's beloved sphynx cat |

Friends and village folk

Margaret Mogg	Owner of the Penberthy Floss village shop
Pierre Rousseau	Owner of Pierre's Patisserie in Highton Mill
Basil Hobbs	Documentary filmmaker and neighbour
Ana Hobbs (nee Barkov)	Former prima ballerina and neighbour

School staff and students

Miss Arabella Critchley	Head teacher
Mrs Ethel Bottomley	Teacher at Ellery Prep
Mr Roderick Smee	New Year One teacher
Angus Archibald	Friend in Clementine's class
Joshua Tribble	Boy in Clementine's class

Araminta Hobbs	Ten-year-old daughter of Basil and Ana
Teddy Hobbs	Five-year-old twin son of Basil and Ana, classmate
Tilda Hobbs	Five-year-old twin daughter of Basil and Ana, classmate

Others

Miss Abigail Richardson, Mr and Mrs Morley, Mr and Mrs Biggins, Polly	Guests at Penberthy House

ABOUT
THE AUTHOR

Jacqueline Harvey taught for many years in girls' boarding schools. She is the author of the bestselling Alice-Miranda series and the Clementine Rose series, and was awarded Honour Book in the 2006 Australian CBC Awards for her picture book *The Sound of the Sea*. She now writes full-time and is working on more Alice-Miranda and Clementine Rose adventures.

www.jacquelineharvey.com.au

Look out for Clementine Rose's next adventure

1 January 2015

Puzzles, quizzes and yummy things to cook

THE
CLEMENTINE
ROSE

Busy Day Book

Out now